My First Graphic Novel

THE KICKBALL KIDS

My First Graphic Novels are published by Stone Arch Books
151 Good Counsel Drive, P.O. Box 669
Mankato, Minnesota 56002
www.stonearchbooks.com

Library of Congress Cataloging-in-Publication Data
Meister, Cari.
 The Kickball Kids / by Cari Meister; illustrated by Julie Olson
 p. cm. — (My First Graphic Novel)
 ISBN 978-1-4342-1294-8 (library binding)
 ISBN 978-1-4342-1410-2 (pbk.)
 1. Graphic novels. [1. Graphic novels. 2. Kickball—Fiction.] I. Olson, Julie, 1976–
ill. II. Title.
PZ7.7.M45Ki 2009
[E]—dc22   2008031969

Summary: Kyle's team is ready for the kickball tournament. They have
practiced kicking, catching, and running. Find out how Kyle's team
does in the big tournament.

Art Director: Heather Kindseth
Graphic Designer: Hilary Wacholz

1 2 3 4 5 6 14 13 12 11 10 09

Printed in the United States of America

My FIRST Graphic Novel

THE KICKBALL KIDS

by Cari Meister

illustrated by Julie Olson

STONE ARCH BOOKS
www.stonearchbooks.com

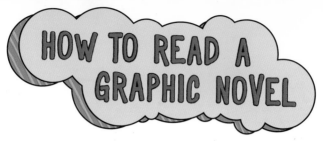

HOW TO READ A GRAPHIC NOVEL

Graphic novels are easy to read. Boxes called panels show you how to follow the story. Look at the panels from left to right and top to bottom.

Read the word boxes and word balloons from left to right as well. Don't forget the sound and action words in the pictures.

The pictures and the words work together to tell the whole story.

Every Saturday, Kyle and his friends met at the park.

They didn't swing. They didn't slide.

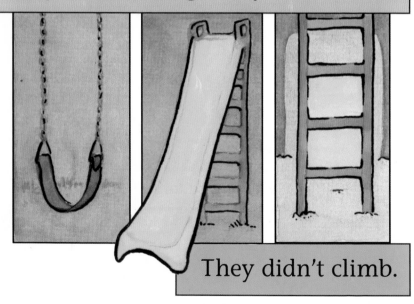

They didn't climb.

Instead, they played kickball.

Kyle was the captain. His team was called the Kicking Kids.

They practiced kicking.

They practiced catching.

They practiced running.

Kyle watched his team.

COMMUNITY KICKBALL
TOURNAMENT

ALL TEAMS WELCOME! GRAB
YOUR KICKBALL AND SIGN UP.
TOURNAMENT STYLE
SINGLE ELIMINATIONS
GAMES BEGIN SOON.

PLEASE CALL

Kyle made the call. He entered
the Kicking Kids in the town
kickball tournament.

The Kicking Kids were the youngest team. But they were good. They beat team after team.

At the end of the day, they were in the finals. They had to play the Super Sharks.

The Sharks rule!

The Sharks were a team of fifth graders.

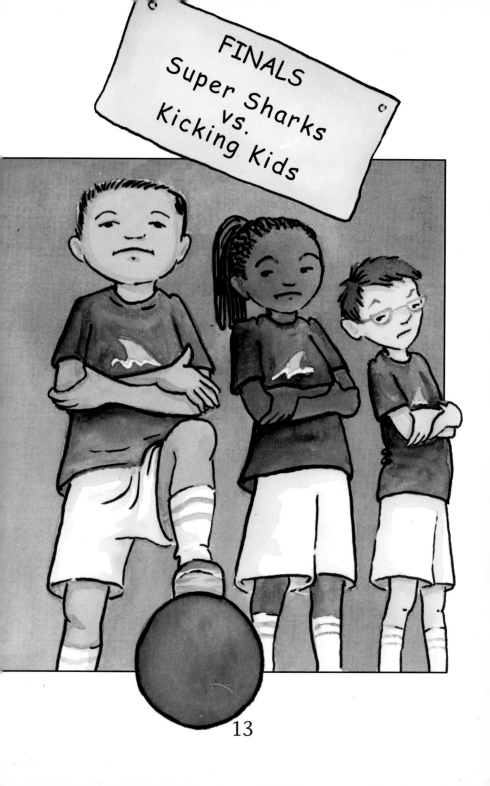

The game went fast. By the final inning, the game was tied. The Kicking Kids were up last.

14

Selena stepped up to the plate.

She kicked the ball
and ran fast.

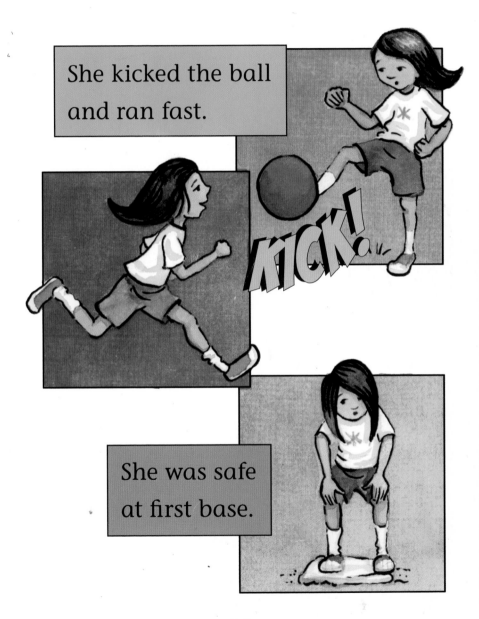

KICK!

She was safe
at first base.

Kyle was next. He never kicked the ball far. But he knew he could run fast.

The first ball rolled in. Kyle missed it. The second ball rolled in. Kyle missed it again. He had one more chance.

The third ball rolled in.

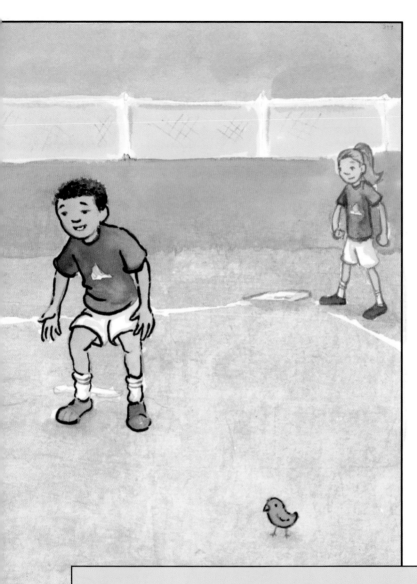

The ball did not go far, but that was okay. Kyle was a fast runner.

Kyle ran and ran and ran.

The other team could not catch him.

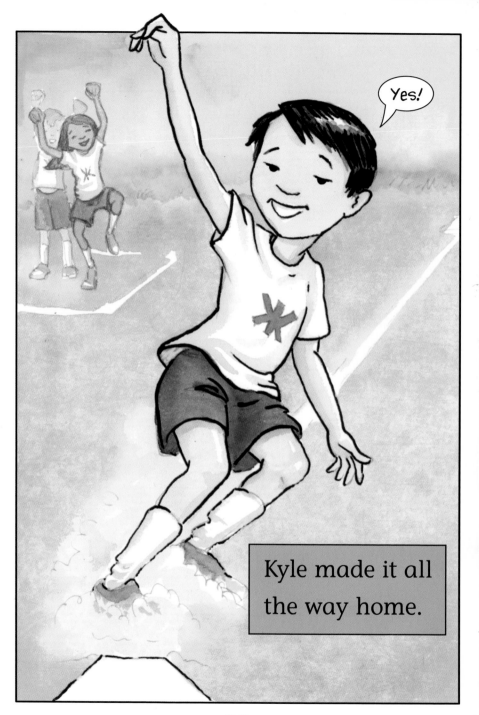

The Kicking Kids won the game!

And they took home the trophy.

The End

ABOUT THE AUTHOR

Cari Meister is the author of many books for children, including the My Pony Jack series and *Luther's Halloween*. She lives on a small farm in Minnesota with her husband, four sons, three horses, one dog, and one cat. Cari enjoys running, snowshoeing, horseback riding, and yoga.

ABOUT THE ILLUSTRATOR

Julie Olson grew up in the middle of six brothers and two sisters, so she learned to play kickball well. Julie found her individuality at home through art. Since then, Julie earned a BFA in illustration, illustrated numerous books for many markets, and started creating her own kickball team with a husband, two sons, and a daughter.

captain (KAP-tuhn)—the leader of the team

foul (foul)—out of bounds

inning (IN-ing)—a part of the game when one team has a turn to kick and the other team is in the outfield; then the teams switch

practice (PRAK-tiss)—to do something over and over

tournament (TUR-nuh-muhnt)—a contest with many different teams playing until one is the winner

DISCUSSION QUESTIONS

1.) Kyle and his friends loved playing kickball. What do you and your friends do together?

2.) Kyle was the captain of the kickball team. Would you like to be captain of a team? Why or why not?

3.) The Kicking Kids had to face older kids in the final game. But Kyle's team was not scared. Have you ever had to face off against older kids? Explain what happened.

WRITING PROMPTS

1.) In this book, the team names were the Kicking Kids and the Super Sharks. If you were the captain, what would you name your team? Write at least three names down.

2.) After the Kicking Kids won the big game, they got a trophy. Draw a picture of a trophy you would want to win.

3.) Throughout the book, there are sound and action words next to some of the art. Pick at least two of those words. Then write your own sentences using those words.

THE FIRST STEP INTO GRAPHIC NOVELS

My FIRST Graphic Novel

These books are the perfect introduction to the world of safe, appealing graphic novels. Each story uses familiar topics, repeating patterns, and core vocabulary words appropriate for a beginning reader. Combine the entertaining story with comic book panels, exciting action elements, and bright colors and a safe graphic novel is born.

INTERNET SITES

Do you want to know more about subjects related to this book? Or are you interested in learning about other topics? Then check out FactHound, a fun, easy way to find Internet sites.

Our investigative staff has already sniffed out great sites for you!

Here's how to use FactHound:

1. Visit *www.facthound.com*

2. Select your grade level.

3. To learn more about subjects related to this book, type in the book's ISBN number: 1434212947.

4. Click the Fetch It button.

FactHound will fetch the best Internet sites for you!